Disney

Finding Tinker Bell

a Never Girls adventure

to the forgotten castle

written by Kiki Thorpe

illustrated by Jana Christy

A STEPPING STONE BOOK™

RANDOM HOUSE 🏠 NEW YORK

Library of Congress Cataloging-in-Publication Data is available upon request.
ISBN 978-0-7364-3955-8 (trade) — ISBN 978-0-7364-8270-7 (lib. bdg.) —
ISBN 978-0-7364-3956-5 (ebook)

rhcbooks.com

Printed in the United States of America

10 9 8 7 6 5 4 3 2 1

This book has been officially leveled by using the F&P Text Level Gradient™ Leveling System.

Never Land...
and Beyond

Far away from the world we know, on the distant Sea of Dreams, lies an island called Never Land. It is a place full of magic, where mermaids sing, fairies play, and children never grow up. Adventures happen every day, and anything is possible.

Though many children have heard of Never Land, only a special few ever find it. The secret, they know, lies not in a set of directions but deep within their hearts, for believing in magic can make extraordinary things happen. It can open doorways you never even knew were there.

One day, through an accident of magic, four special girls found a portal to Never Land right in their own backyard. The enchanted island became the girls' secret playground, one they visited every chance they got. With the fairies of Pixie Hollow as their friends and guides, they made many magical discoveries.

But Never Land isn't the only island on the Sea of Dreams. When a special friend goes missing, the girls set out across the sea to find her. Beyond the shores of Never Land, they encounter places far stranger than they ever could have imagined. . . .

This is their story.

Shadow Island

Forgotten
Castle

Chapter 1

"There's Tinker Bell! I see her!" With a shout of excitement, Gabby Vasquez plunged into the shallow river. She splashed through knee-deep water toward the reeds on the other side.

Gabby's older sister, Mia Vasquez, and their friends Kate McCrady and Lainey Winters waited on the bank with four fairies. They all watched as Gabby parted the reeds.

A startled duck flapped into the air.

"Never mind!" Gabby turned to wade back. "It was just a duck."

Kate arched an eyebrow. "No kidding."

"It sure looked like Tinker Bell, though," Gabby added as she climbed, dripping, onto the bank.

They were searching for the fairy Tinker Bell. Their journey had taken them from Never Land to the strange Shadow Island. After days of looking, the fairy Fawn had finally spotted Tink's boat by a waterfall. But the boat was gone before they could catch up with it. Now they were following the river downstream, hoping it would lead them to her.

Gabby had her own reason for wanting to find Tinker Bell. The *Treasure*, the toy boat Tink was sailing, belonged to her family. Her great-grandfather had made it, and Gabby had promised Papi she would bring it home safe and sound.

But looking hard for something can play tricks on your mind. The longer Gabby searched for Tink, the more she thought that she saw her everywhere. Just that day, she'd mistaken a goldfinch for the fairy's golden glow. A glimmer Gabby was sure was Tink had turned out to be a large dragonfly. And now the duck.

Fawn, the animal-talent fairy, shook her head. "Sorry, Gabby, but how could you mistake a *duck* for Tinker Bell?"

"Well, Tink is in a boat," Gabby replied. "And the duck was the same size as the boat. And its feathers were sort of greenish, and . . ." She trailed off. They were all staring at her.

"Um, they both float?" she finished meekly.

"Gabby," Mia said with a sigh, "that's the third wild-goose chase today."

"Don't you mean a wild-*duck* chase?" Kate said with a smirk.

Mia rolled her eyes. "I'm serious. Gabby, you have to stop messing around. At this rate, we'll be going in circles on Shadow Island forever."

"I wasn't messing around," Gabby muttered.

"Just do us a favor," Mia said. "Next time, don't yell 'Tinker Bell' unless you're sure it's her."

Gabby pressed her lips tight together.

She hated it when Mia talked down to her, especially in front of the fairies. Of course she wouldn't yell "Tinker Bell" unless she was sure! Or, at least, really and truly *almost* sure. Did they think she was making stuff up *on purpose*?

Gabby scowled at the reeds where the duck had been hiding. "Dumb duck," she grumbled.

Silvermist, the water-talent fairy, eyed Gabby's soaked tutu. "You've probably washed off your fairy dust. You'll need more to fly."

Silvermist didn't sound upset, but Gabby heard the gentle reprimand. She knew that they were trying to save fairy dust. The fairy dust allowed them all to fly, and it gave the fairies their magic. But they only had a small supply. They'd already learned the hard way that they had to make it last.

"It's okay," she said quickly. "I can walk."

Gabby glanced at the other fairies to make sure they'd heard. But they weren't paying any attention. They were huddled over the map of Shadow Island. Their wings gently stirred the air as they studied it.

"What I don't understand is where else she could be," Fawn said. "This is the only river. I can't believe Tink is that far ahead of us."

"Maybe there's a branch of the river that we missed," Rosetta, the garden-talent fairy, suggested.

Iridessa, the light-talent fairy, eyed the dark clouds gathering on the horizon. "I'm worried about those thunderheads. What we should be looking for is a place to get out of the rain," she said.

Gabby tried to look over the fairies' shoulders at the map. But they glanced up, frowning.

"Sweet girl, would you mind stepping back? You're casting a shadow," Rosetta said.

"Sorry." Gabby moved away.

With nothing better to do, she sat down beside the stream. The water made a pretty sound as it ran over the rocks. Tiny fish darted in the shallows.

Gabby watched as a small dark shape flitted over the surface of the water. It disappeared into the reeds on the other side of the stream.

Gabby had seen it before. It looked like a small bird or a large moth. Whatever it was, it had been following them for a while.

"There's that moth again," she announced to no one in particular.

No one gave any sign that they'd heard her.

Gabby watched the reeds. A moment

later, the moth appeared again a short distance away. *It has an odd shape,* Gabby thought. It was not really mothlike at all. In fact, it looked a little like a fairy.

She opened her mouth to say so, then thought better of it. "Sure is a funny-looking moth, though."

Fawn finally glanced up from the map. "Moth?"

"Never mind. It's gone." Gabby looked toward the trees where the moth had disappeared. Beyond the tree branches, she spied something she hadn't noticed before.

Gabby squinted at it. "Hey," she said.

"I think I saw a cave a little ways back," Kate was saying. "We could wait out the storm there."

"Hey, guys," Gabby said again.

"Maybe we're better off stopping here for the night," Fawn said. "We could find a tree to shelter under."

"Or," Gabby said loudly, "we could try that castle."

This time, they all looked up. "What castle?" asked Kate.

"There." Gabby pointed. Rising above the trees was a tall stone tower.

Chapter 2

The castle sat in a clearing, overlooking the sea. It was very old. Whole sections of it had collapsed. The walls that remained were weather-beaten and spotted with lichen. The tower they'd seen through the trees was so covered in vines it looked as if it had grown up from the earth, like some sort of ancient tree.

And yet, the sunlight breaking through the clouds struck the castle with a golden light, so that the stones seemed to glow. To Gabby and her friends, peering from the edge of the forest, the castle looked like something straight out of a fairy tale.

"It's abandoned," Mia said. She sounded both disappointed and relieved.

"Maybe, maybe not," Lainey whispered. "There could be a magical princess asleep in that tower."

Gabby looked up, her eyes widening "Really?"

Lainey smiled. "I was only kidding, Gabby." She glanced back at the castle, then added, "Sort of," under her breath.

"What are we waiting for?" Kate said. "Come on. Let's check it out!"

"Hold on." Mia caught Kate's sleeve

before she could rise into the air. "What if it's haunted?"

"Let's hope it is," Kate replied with a devilish grin. "That will make things even more interesting."

She flew off toward the castle. After a moment's hesitation, Mia, Lainey, and the fairies followed.

"Wait for me!" Gabby cried, chasing after them. Without fairy dust, she had to run to keep up.

Halfway across the clearing, they came to a great stone archway. It had clearly once been some sort of gateway or entrance. But the wall that had held it was long gone. Now only the arch remained.

Kate, Mia, Lainey, and the fairies flew right over it without stopping. But to

Gabby, standing below, the arch made a grand impression. She paused before it.

The low sun was behind her. It cast the shadow of the arch across the ground. Gabby could see her own shadow framed within it. The wings she always wore looked almost real, as if she were truly a fairy.

Gabby started forward. But just as she was about to pass beneath the arch, something flitted past her face, making her draw up short.

That strange moth again! What was it doing here?

The moth had disappeared. But a moment later it was back. This time it flew so close it nearly brushed her nose.

"Hey! Buzz off!" Gabby waved a hand, trying to swat it away. Why was it

bothering her?

"Gabby!" Mia called. She was standing near the main part of the castle. Lainey and Kate had already disappeared inside. "Are you coming?"

"Yes!" Gabby ran toward her.

As Gabby stepped through the arch, she felt a gentle snap, as if something stretched tightly had broken loose. In the same instant, a strange feeling came over her. A sad, anxious feeling, as if she'd lost something important.

She checked the pockets of the shorts she wore under her tutu. She felt for her fairy wings on her back. Everything seemed to be in place. But the strange feeling did not go away.

"Gabby?" Mia was starting to sound impatient.

"Coming!" Gabby brushed off the feeling, and ran to join her friends.

She found Mia standing before a crumbling entryway. Up close, the castle looked even more desolate. Most of the roof was gone, and whole walls were missing. Weeds grew where the floors had been. The tower was the only section that hadn't crumbled. The vines appeared to be holding it together.

"Who do you think lived here?" Lainey asked as they wandered among the empty rooms.

"Kings and queens, obviously," Mia said. "Probably a whole royal court."

"But that's what's so strange," Lainey replied. "We haven't seen any people on Shadow Island. So what happened to them?"

"Maybe they got tired of living here and moved somewhere nicer," Kate said.

"Like Florida," said Gabby. "That's where the Johnsons moved when they got tired."

"You mean, RE-tired." Mia gave her a look. "Kings and queens don't move to Florida. Florida didn't even exist when this place was built."

"I know what Gabby means, though," Kate said. "If you spent your whole life on Shadow Island, you'd probably really want to retire somewhere else."

They climbed through the ruins, scrambling over old walls and through narrow passageways. There was no trace of whoever had lived there. But it was thrilling to imagine that kings and queens had once passed exactly where their feet were walking now.

Navigating through the ruins was a little like being in a maze. Soon Gabby lost sight of Mia and the older girls. As she came around a corner, she saw Iridessa hovering near a window, frowning.

"What's wrong?" Gabby asked.

Iridessa jumped, as if she'd been deep in thought. "Oh, nothing, Gabby. I was just looking at the light. Something's not right here, don't you think?"

Gabby looked out the window. She didn't see anything strange. "I'm not sure."

"Maybe it's nothing," Iridessa said. "I'm probably just—"

Suddenly, a scream echoed across the castle grounds. Iridessa gasped.

"That sounded like Mia!" Gabby exclaimed.

They raced toward the sound. Outside the exterior castle wall, they spotted a small building shaped like a beehive. Mia came bursting out the door of it, waving her hands over her head.

"Ugh!" she cried. "They were everywhere!"

"What was?" Lainey asked. She'd come running up with the rest of the fairies.

"Bats." Kate emerged from the little building Mia had just come out of. "This place is full of them."

"Bats? Is that all?" Fawn snorted. "The way you were screaming, I thought you'd met a ghost."

"They were in my hair!" Mia touched her thick black curls and  shuddered. She turned to Kate. "You told me there would be doves in there."

"Well, it's called a dovecote. I learned about it in a book on castles. There *were* doves in there, once upon a time," Kate said with a shrug. "I guess when the doves moved out, the bats moved in."

"I want to see them!" said Lainey, who adored animals of every kind. She started toward the squat little building. But Fawn stopped her.

"No, don't. You'll upset them more. Mia probably already scared them half to death with her screaming," the animal-talent fairy said.

"They scared *me* half to death," Mia replied.

Kate glanced toward the dovecote. "Don't look now, but they're coming back for revenge."

"Very funny," Mia said. But the words were barely out of her mouth when a small, winged shape darted through the air over her head. Another was right behind it.

"Eeee!" Mia screamed, and flapped her arms again. "Help! The bats are coming to get me!"

"Stop screaming," Fawn commanded. "They're not coming to get *you.* They're coming to get their dinner. Look."

More bats were flying out of the low door of the dovecote. At the same moment, the girls noticed that the sun, which seemingly moments before had been in the sky, was slipping below the horizon. They heard a rumble of thunder.

"Now what are we going to do?"

Silvermist asked.

"Well," said Kate, "I have always wanted to sleep in a castle."

Chapter 3

From a castle window, Iridessa watched a flock of crows. They were circling above the forest, just beyond the castle grounds.

Iridessa could tell they were crows by their color—the birds were black as night. Still, there was something odd about them.

Not just odd. Wrong, Iridessa thought. Something about the birds didn't look right.

"Fawn," she said, "do you see those crows over there?"

Fawn looked where Iridessa was pointing. "They don't look like crows."

Iridessa nodded. "But why not?"

"They're too fat. And their heads are too round. They look more like pigeons to me," Fawn said.

Ah, that was it. They were the wrong shape. "And another thing," Fawn went on. "Crows are noisy. These birds haven't made a sound."

"So they're pigeons, then?" Iridessa asked.

"Maybe." Fawn looked unsure. She glanced at Iridessa. "What's bothering you?"

"This place is bothering me," Iridessa

admitted. "But I can't put my finger on why exactly. It's just a . . . "

She was about to say "a gut feeling." But she stopped herself. Normally, Iridessa didn't put any stock in gut feelings. She was not a superstitious fairy. She didn't believe in fables or myths. Of course, she had magic like any fairy. But it was *sensible* magic. A light fairy's gift was for shining light in the darkness, for making things clear and bright. The only gut feeling she paid any attention to was the grumbling of her empty stomach.

But when Iridessa thought of spending the night in the castle, the uneasy feeling only grew stronger.

"It's just that it's cold," Iridessa told Fawn, "and dark." Compared to sleeping under the stars, the castle seemed chilly and bleak.

The girls, however, all seemed thrilled at the prospect of sleeping in the tower. "A castle slumber party!" Mia exclaimed.

Gabby clapped her hands. "We'll be like princesses!"

Iridessa would rather have slept in an open meadow, with poppy petals for bedding and fireflies for a night-light. But as the first drops of rain spattered down, she realized they had no choice. They would have to make the best of it.

Murmuring with excitement, the girls climbed the stone steps into the tower.

Iridessa followed reluctantly.

Inside, they looked around. The room was bare and sunk in gloom. The tiny windows let in little of the fading daylight.

Mia's face fell. "This isn't quite what I was picturing," she said.

Lainey examined the great stone hearth. It was nearly as tall as she was. "I wish we had a fire," she said, "or at least some candles."

"Who needs firelight when you have *fairy* light?" Iridessa said.

The fairies all brightened their glows. Instantly, the room filled with cozy light.

"We'll need beds, too." Rosetta fluttered down to floor level. She skimmed over the stones until she found what she was looking for—a small patch of moss growing in the corner.

Rosetta sprinkled fairy dust on the moss. Then she raised her hands and beckoned to it.

"Come to me, good little moss," she murmured.

As they watched, the moss started to grow. It spread across the stone floor, slowly at first. Then it grew faster and faster. Soon it had covered the whole room like a plush green carpet.

Rosetta waved her hand again. Tiny white flowers sprouted from the moss.

"Ta-da! Flower beds!" Rosetta said with a flourish.

The girls clapped. The fairies did, too. Iridessa smiled at her friend. Even though

she was used to Rosetta's gardening magic, the light fairy never got tired of seeing it. "It's lovely," she said to Rosetta.

Rosetta shrugged. "I have to practice when I can. I wouldn't want the flowers in Pixie Hollow to think I'd lost my touch."

They settled down on the soft bedding. But although they were tired from the long day, no one seemed ready to close her eyes.

"Look." Lainey pointed to the wall, where Iridessa's glow cast a circle of light. "Kate's shadow looks like a whale."

Kate was lying on her stomach with her feet up in the air. Her legs did look a bit like a whale's tail.

"*Pssshh!*" Kate pretended to spout.

Mia held her hands up to the light so they made the shadow of a rabbit. "I can make a bunny!"

"Watch out, bunny. Here comes a dog." Lainey made a shadow dog with her hands. It chased Mia's shadow rabbit around the wall.

"And here comes a hawk!" Kate said. She made her hands into the shadow of a bird.

"Oh, I have one!" Gabby joined them, holding her hands up to the light. "Look, I'm a—"

She broke off, staring. "Where's my shadow?" she asked.

Where Gabby's shadow should have been, there was only an empty circle of light.

"You must be standing in the wrong place," Mia said. "Move over here."

She positioned Gabby right in front of Iridessa's light. Still Gabby's shadow did not appear.

The other girls tried to help. They moved Gabby here and there. But nothing they did brought her shadow forth.

"Iridessa, make your light brighter," Kate suggested.

"It's not my light that's the problem," the light-talent fairy replied with alarm. Now she knew what had been bothering her since they'd arrived at the castle—it was the shadows. They appeared where they should not have been. And where they should have been, they were not.

"Where's my shadow?" Gabby repeated. She was growing upset. "What's happened to it?"

"Nothing's happened." Mia put a protective arm around her sister's shoulders. "I'm sure there's a reasonable explanation. Right, Iridessa?"

"Hmm," Iridessa said.

She fluttered around Gabby, looking at her first from one side, then the other. But no matter which way Iridessa shone her light, the girl didn't cast a shadow.

"There can be only one explanation," Iridessa concluded. "Gabby, you've lost your shadow."

Mia frowned. "When I said there must be a reasonable explanation, that is not what I had in mind!"

"Will I get it back?" Gabby asked.

"I'm not sure," Iridessa admitted. "Since we don't know where it's gone."

Gabby's lower lip trembled. "I'll be the only kid in kindergarten without a shadow!"

"Iridessa," Mia said, "may I speak to you for a moment?" She stepped to the far side of the room and beckoned for Iridessa to join. "Do you see how upset

Gabby is?" Mia whispered when they were alone.

"I do." Iridessa nodded. "Poor thing. It must be quite a shock."

"Iridessa!" Mia hissed. "You're the one upsetting her. Why would you tell her she lost her shadow?"

"Because she obviously has," Iridessa replied.

"But . . . but . . ." Mia waved her arms in frustration. "Shadows don't just come off!"

"Mia," Iridessa said calmly, "since we've come to Shadow Island, we've met talking trees. We've seen a turtle the size of a small island. We followed mist horses across the sky."

"So?" said Mia.

"So I think it's safe to say that anything is possible," Iridessa replied. "There is powerful magic at work here. I've felt it since we arrived."

Now Mia looked worried. "What kind of magic?"

"I don't know yet. And unless you want to upset Gabby more, please don't say anything until we can figure it out."

Mia pressed her lips together and nodded.

Iridessa flew over to Gabby. "It's going to be okay. I'm sure we'll find your shadow in the morning. Now, it's been a long day and we all need sleep. Fawn, Silvermist, Rosetta?"

The fairies fluttered up. "Yes, Iridessa?" said Fawn.

"We'll take turns staying awake. I'll take the first shift." She smiled at Gabby. "For tonight, consider us your own personal night-lights."

chapter 4

Deep in the night, Iridessa woke with a start.

She blinked in the darkness. Rosetta, the last fairy on watch, had drifted off. All the other fairies were asleep, too. Without the light from their glows, the room was nearly pitch black.

Iridessa flared her own glow to see better. What had awakened her?

She could make out the dark forms of
the girls sleeping on the floor. She counted
one, two, three—

Only three! Someone was missing!

She flew to the doorway and looked out.
The rain had stopped. The ruins looked
pale in the light of a half-moon. Had one

of the girls ventured out alone into the night?

Just then, Iridessa heard a soft noise, like a foot scuffing against stone. It was coming from within the tower.

Iridessa followed the sound. At the back of the tower, she came to a spiraling stone stairway. Halfway up the stairs, Gabby was standing on tiptoe, looking out a small window.

"Gabby?" Iridessa whispered.

Gabby gasped and spun around.

"Iridessa, you scared me," she said.

"What are you doing up?" Iridessa asked.

"I thought I heard something outside," Gabby told her. "I wanted to see what it was."

"What did it sound like?" Iridessa asked.

"It was hard to tell. Sort of like a bell, I guess," Gabby said.

"A bell? Are you sure?" Iridessa was struck with sudden hope. Clumsies sometimes thought fairy voices sounded like bells. Had Gabby heard Tink's voice? "Could it have been a fairy?"

"It didn't sound like a fairy. It was different," Gabby replied.

"Different how?" Iridessa pressed.

Gabby thought about it. "It was slower. And sadder," she explained.

Iridessa looked out the window. She could see the castle ruins, shrouded in mist, and the dense, dark forest beyond. All was still and quiet. "Maybe you dreamed it," she told Gabby.

"Maybe," Gabby agreed sleepily. Her eyelids were starting to droop.

"Why don't you go back to sleep?" Iridessa suggested. "It's been a long day, and we both could use some rest."

"All right," Gabby agreed.

As they turned to go, Iridessa cast one last glance outside. Her heart skipped a beat.

On the far side of the castle grounds, she saw an immense shape that hadn't been there before. It was formless, like a great cloud, and blacker than the night itself. It seemed to blot out any sign of the forest beyond.

Iridessa blinked. When she looked again, it was gone. She could see the forest lit by moonlight.

"Iridessa?" Gabby called to her. "Are you coming?"

"Yes." Iridessa came away from the window. Gabby shuffled back to her mossy bed. Iridessa was silent as she lit the way, but her mind churned.

What could that thing have been? Were her eyes playing tricks on her? Or had she really seen something out there in the night?

Gabby's eyes were closing even as her head touched down. "Night, Iridessa."

"Good night, Gabby."

Iridessa flew to her own little tuft of moss. But she couldn't

fall asleep. Her glow, usually so strong and steady, was flickering like a candle. Iridessa realized it was because she was trembling.

Chapter 5

For the rest of the night, Iridessa lay awake. Her mind went over and over the strange shape in the darkness.

It was too big to be an animal, at least any sort of animal Iridessa had seen before. But she did not think it had been just a cloud or a patch of mist. It had moved in a lumbering, animal-like way. What was it?

Iridessa decided not to tell her friends what she had seen. She didn't want to frighten them for no reason. But she knew that she had to find out more.

When the first rays of light touched the sky, Iridessa rose. She flew over the sleeping girls and fairies and out of the castle.

Dawn made a rosy band of light on the horizon. The air was cool and fresh. Iridessa breathed in deeply.

Most light-talent fairies loved the night because that was when they shone brightest. But morning was Iridessa's favorite time of day. It was a time to put things in order and start fresh.

Across the castle grounds, she could see the lone stone archway standing among the tall grass and wildflowers and, beyond it, the dark forest. This was where Iridessa had seen the dark shape in the night. It was where she headed now.

In the early-morning light, the clearing seemed quiet and peaceful. Iridessa searched all around for tracks. But she found nothing, not even a bent blade of grass. There was no sign that anything large had passed that way.

Had she only imagined it? In the light of day, her fears faded a little. Perhaps it had been nothing after all—a trick of the moonlight, maybe.

The sun rose above the treetops and touched the meadow. Iridessa plucked up a sunbeam and squeezed it between

her hands. Its warmth made her feel calm and strong. Morning light was not the brightest. But it had its own magic. It held all the promise of a new day.

The grass rustled behind her. Iridessa dropped the sunbeam and spun around.

Gabby was standing there.

"Oh," Iridessa sighed. "Gabby, what are you doing out here?"

"I followed you," Gabby said. "What are *you* doing?"

Iridessa hesitated. Should she tell Gabby about the strange thing she'd seen in the night?

No, better not to mention it, she decided. Poor Gabby already had enough to worry about with her missing shadow.

"I like to get up early," Iridessa said. She

plucked up another sunbeam and rolled it between her hands.

"Can you show me how to do that?" Gabby asked.

"Do what?" asked Iridessa.

"Hold the light."

Iridessa was about to say no. Only light-talent fairies could grasp a sunbeam. Even for them, it took practice. But Gabby looked so hopeful, so eager. What harm was there in trying?

"All right. Hold out your hands. No, like this." Iridessa turned her palms to the sky.

Then she shook fairy dust from her wings into Gabby's open hands. The fairy dust wouldn't give Gabby light talent. But it might help a little.

Iridessa plucked another sunbeam from the air. She formed it into a glowing ball. Ever so gently, she placed the ball in Gabby's hands.

Light from the ball cast a golden glow across Gabby's excited face. But as soon as she tried to close her hands around it, the light faded away.

"Not bad for a Clumsy," Iridessa said.

"You might have a little light magic in you after all."

Gabby's whole face lit up. "Really? Do you think so?"

Iridessa smiled. "It's possible."

"Let me try again!" Gabby said.

Iridessa collected another sunbeam. But this time, when she put it in Gabby's waiting hands, it bounced off and shot away into the grass.

"Oh!" Iridessa gasped. A dark cloud of butterflies rose where it landed.

"Look at them all!" Gabby exclaimed as the butterflies whirled over their heads. "Have you ever seen so many?"

The butterflies scattered across the open field. Iridessa saw that the meadow was full of butterflies, many of them gray or black. Looking closer, she realized why. They were shadows!

Shadows without objects, Iridessa thought. It seemed Gabby wasn't the only one who'd lost her shadow. Something was causing the shadows to come off.

"Gabby!" she said. "Did you walk through this field yesterday?"

Gabby nodded. "My fairy dust washed off in the stream, remember? I was running to catch up with you guys."

It has something to do with this meadow, Iridessa thought. That would explain why Gabby had lost her shadow, when the rest of them had not. Did a strange type of grass grow there? Or some kind of poisonous flower?

At that moment, a white butterfly

flitted past. Iridessa decided to follow it. She watched it closely as it weaved through the meadow. When it flew under the archway, the butterfly seemed to struggle for a moment, as if it were caught in an invisible spider web.

A second later, it flew on—leaving its shadow behind.

It's the arch! Iridessa thought. *Somehow the shadow comes off when someone goes through! But why?*

Iridessa watched the left-behind shadow. Alone, the shadow moved in a panicky way. It darted left and right. It looked as if it was searching for something to grab on to.

"Iridessa, come look at this!" Gabby called.

Iridessa flew over to her. A little black cloud was drifting over the grass. It looked almost like a rain cloud, but smaller and denser.

"What is it?" Gabby asked.

"I don't know. Don't touch—" Iridessa started to say. But Gabby was already reaching out a finger to poke it.

Her finger slid into the cloud and vanished. Gabby gasped and jerked her hand back. Her finger reappeared.

"What is it?" Gabby repeated.

"Another shadow!" Iridessa realized. A shadow so dark they couldn't see through it. But what could have made it?

A butterfly shadow flitted toward them, its wings flapping frantically. When it came near the dark cloud, it swerved toward it. For a moment, they could still see the outline of its wings. Then it disappeared into the shadowy mass.

"Hmm." Iridessa suddenly had an idea.

She plucked a sunbeam from the air and rolled it between her hands until it formed a narrow wand. Carefully, she reached out and touched the shadow with the ray of light.

As the light pierced it, the cloud broke apart. The shadows of a hundred butterflies rose into the air.

Gabby gaped in amazement. Together they watched the shadows swirl above them. "How did you know it would do that?"

"I didn't, really," Iridessa replied. "It

was just a hunch. But look—see how the shadows follow each other?" Already the freed butterfly shadows were joining together again, forming dark-winged clumps in the air. "It's as if they can't bear to be alone."

"They miss their butterflies," Gabby said.

"Gabby, you know, I think you're right." Iridessa was surprised at how perceptive Gabby was. It hadn't occurred to Iridessa to wonder *why* the shadows clung together. But she saw that it made perfect sense. The shadows longed to be attached to something, even if it was only to each other.

"Do you think my shadow misses me?" Gabby asked.

"I'm sure it does," Iridessa said. "And now we are one step closer to finding it. We learned something today that we didn't know before."

"What's that?" Gabby asked.

"Shadows are not always what they seem," Iridessa said.

chapter 6

Like most people, Gabby had never paid much attention to her shadow. But as she followed Iridessa back to the castle, she found she missed it quite a bit. Without her shadow, Gabby felt as if she weren't quite connected to the ground. Any moment, it seemed, she might float away like a balloon. It was an unpleasant feeling.

When they reached the tower, they

found the other girls and fairies sitting outside. They were having a picnic of walnuts, pears, and tiny strawberries.

"My! Where did all this come from?" Iridessa asked as she fluttered up.

"Mia and I found them growing nearby," Rosetta said. "The strawberries are wild. But pear and walnut trees don't usually grow in forests like this. They must be left over from the old kingdom."

"It's funny to think that the trees lasted longer than the people," Lainey said.

"Where were you guys?" Kate asked as Gabby and Iridessa sat down and helped themselves to breakfast.

"We were doing a bit of sleuthing," Iridessa replied. "It turns out Gabby's not

the only one around here who's missing a shadow." She told them about the butterfly shadows and the stone arch. "We think that might be where Gabby lost her shadow."

"Just like those shadows we saw in the woods on Misty Peak!" Lainey said. "Remember the wolf shadow that followed us?"

They all shivered. "How could we forget?" Mia said.

"The question is: Why?" Fawn said. "What's causing the shadows to come off?"

"It has something to do with these ruins," Iridessa replied. "I've felt it since we got here. Strange magic hangs over this place."

"I wish we had a book," Mia said, "or

something that could tell us about this castle."

"We do!" Fawn said, suddenly flying to her feet. "Oh, why didn't I think of it before? The bats!"

Mia looked confused. "The bats have a book?" she asked.

"No, of course not," Fawn said impatiently. "But they'll know the story of this place. They're incredibly smart, perceptive creatures. And they are wonderful storytellers. Their oral histories go back generations. If anyone can tell us about the shadows, the bats can."

"Let's go right now!" Iridessa flew up to join Fawn.

The girls started to get up, too. But

Fawn stopped them. "We can't all go barging into their home," she said.

"I was thinking the same thing," Mia said, quickly sitting back down.

"Iridessa and I will go," Fawn said. "And you too, Gabby."

"Me?" Gabby's heart sank. She wasn't sure she wanted to meet a bunch of spooky bats. Especially not without Mia there to hold her hand.

"I'll come," Lainey volunteered. "I'd love to see the bats."

"Me, too," said Kate, who hated to be left out of anything.

"No, just us three," Fawn said firmly. "Too many people will disturb them. And if they get upset, they won't talk to us."

Gabby wished she could trade places

with Lainey. But she followed Fawn and Iridessa to the small round building where the bats lived.

Outside the door, Fawn paused. "Now, remember, let me do the talking. Don't make sudden movements. Bats don't use echolocation in their homes. So if you start jumping around, they're likely to bump into you."

"Got it," Gabby said, nodding hard.

"And, Iridessa," Fawn said, "try not to shine too brightly. They're very sensitive to light."

Iridessa dimmed her glow a notch. "Fawn, are you sure about this?" she asked. "How do we know that they won't take us for giant fireflies and try to eat us?"

"They won't do that, will they, Fawn?"

Gabby asked. She couldn't stand it if anything bad happened to one of the fairies.

"No," said Fawn. "At least, I don't think so. They prefer mosquitoes. Everybody ready?"

Iridessa squared her shoulders. "Let's do this."

Fawn flew into the darkened doorway, with Iridessa and Gabby following close behind.

At once, Gabby noticed the smell—a rank odor that reminded her of the zoo back home. She covered her nose and breathed through her mouth as they moved farther into the room.

When they reached what Gabby guessed was the center of the building, they stopped. The air above them was filled with rustling, flapping sounds. Fawn pointed toward the ceiling.

Gabby looked up and gasped. *There must be hundreds of them!*

The bats hung upside down on the ceiling. They looked packed so tightly

that when one shifted, the movement rippled across the whole colony. They looked like a living, breathing, seething canopy. The sight of it made Gabby's skin crawl.

Fawn fluttered up to a bunch. She squeaked something in Bat. But the bats turned away from her glow. They burrowed into each other, grumbling.

Fawn tried the next group. As the light of her glow touched them, the bats covered their eyes, complaining. Gabby didn't understand Bat language, but she could guess what they were saying. *Leave us alone! We're trying to sleep.*

Fawn tried another bunch, and the same thing happened.

Gabby and Iridessa exchanged worried

looks. What if they couldn't wake up the bats?

Just then, one of the smaller bats broke away from the ceiling. It fluttered toward them.

"Ah!" Fawn smiled. "I knew we'd find it eventually."

"Find what?" Gabby whispered.

"The night owl. Or I guess you could call it the morning bat. It's the bat who's wide-awake when everyone else is sleeping. There's one in every colony," Fawn replied.

The bat came into the dim light of the fairies' glows. It was the size of a mouse, but its wings made it seem bigger. It had

huge ears and needle-like fangs. But as it came closer, Gabby saw that its eyes were intelligent and kind.

Fawn and the bat squeaked back and forth for several long moments. Then the bat flew away.

"Well?" Iridessa whispered. "What did it say?"

"We were just saying hello," Fawn replied.

"*That* was hello?" Gabby said. They'd been talking for a few minutes!

"Bats are very formal," Fawn explained. "You can't rush greetings. It's considered quite rude. But I have good news. She says she's happy to tell us the history of this castle."

"But where did she go?" Iridessa asked.

The bat had disappeared into the darkness near the ceiling.

"She has to wake her family," Fawn said. "Bats have a particular way of telling stories. It's more like a conversation. They all play a role in remembering. Oh, look. Here they come."

A group of about a dozen bats was fluttering down toward them. When they reached Fawn and her friends, Gabby thought they would land. But instead, the bats remained in the air, circling above their heads and squeaking faintly.

With Fawn translating, the bats began to tell the story of the forgotten castle.

Chapter 7

The Bats' Story

Long, long ago, a king ruled over this island. He was a powerful man, who had conquered many lands. It is said that he never lost a battle. But he was neither wise nor brave. He had come to power through wicked means—the source of his strength was a magic stone.

The king had gathered a great fortune, but he felt no peace. He lived in fear that someone would steal his stone—and his throne. His fear became so immense that he fled to a remote island, taking only his servants. He built a fortress to protect his stone. And with its magic power, he cast a spell over the island so that it might never be found.

But even this was not enough. Day after day, alone in his castle, the king's madness grew. No one escaped his suspicion. He even began to fear his own shadow.

His shadow tormented him. It followed him everywhere. He could not be rid of it. At night, the king woke in terror, certain that someone was in the room. When he lit a candle, he saw that it was his shadow.

The king vowed to be rid of shadows. Of course, no one paid him much mind. He was mad, after all.

But then one night, from the king's

window, there came a blinding flash. A shudder ran through the castle, as if it might split in two. The king emerged from his chambers, wild-eyed, and announced that he had banished all shadows from his home. His shadow would never trouble him again.

From then on, no creature—human or animal—cast a shadow within the castle walls.

The troubled servants whispered of witchcraft and abandoned him. The king didn't mind. Alone in his castle, he was finally content.

His peace lasted for three days.

Then a new shadow appeared—a shadow like no other. It was not of a human or an animal, but something far

more frightening—
a great shadow beast.

It was more than
the king could bear. He
fled the island and was never seen again.
His kingdom fell into ruin.

This all happened ages ago. The king is
long gone. But the curse he placed on the
castle remains.

*

The bats were flying slower now. Their
squeaking grew fainter. Gabby could tell
the story was coming to an end. But they
still hadn't answered the most important
question.

"How do I get *my* shadow back?" Gabby
wondered aloud. "Ask them, Fawn."

Fawn repeated the question into the air.

The bats swirled and squeaked. Fawn translated: "They say, 'To undo the curse and make what's halved whole again, you must find the magic stone.'"

A bat swooped toward them, so low Gabby had to duck.

Fawn frowned.

"What's wrong?" Gabby asked.

"They're all talking at once," Fawn told them. "They say, 'Beware.'"

"Beware?" Gabby exclaimed. "Beware of *what*?"

"Shh!" said Iridessa. "Not so loud!"

But it was too late. As Gabby's voice echoed through the quiet chamber, a ripple went through the colony overhead. A cloud of startled bats released from the ceiling.

In an instant, the room filled with squeaking.

The bats' leathery wings brushed against Gabby. She turned and tried to run. But the bats were everywhere. The air was thick with their furry bodies. It was like a *blizzard* of bats.

Gabby couldn't see the door. She couldn't even see where the fairies had gone.

Just then, two bright lights appeared

in front of her. It was Iridessa and Fawn, their glows blazing.

"Quick, follow us! This way!" Fawn cried.

With her arms over her head, Gabby ran after the fairies. The dots of light wove through the room, dodging the swarming bats. Soon she could see a narrow rectangle of light.

A moment later, Gabby plunged into sunlight. After the darkness of the bat house, the daylight was blinding.

Mia, Kate, Lainey, Rosetta, and Silvermist were all gathered there, waiting.

"Well?" asked Kate. "What did they say?"

Chapter 8

"Cursed?" Mia exclaimed. "You mean to tell me we spent the night in a cursed castle?"

The girls and fairies were sitting on stones in the old courtyard as Fawn told the bats' story. Even with the warm sun shining on her, Gabby shivered. The bats' final warning still echoed in her mind: *Beware.*

Beware of what? She and Fawn had left before they could find out.

"Look on the bright side, Mia," said Lainey. "At least the castle isn't haunted."

"Honestly, I'm not sure which is worse," said Mia.

"But we can break the curse. We just have to find that magic stone!" Kate rubbed her hands together. This was the sort of adventure she lived for.

"Oh, sure," Mia said, looking far less excited. "We just have to break a centuries-old curse. No big deal."

"It does seem like a lot of trouble for one little old shadow," Rosetta agreed. "Gabby, are you *sure* you need it? I don't suppose you'd consider leaving it behind?"

"Rosetta!" Silvermist exclaimed.

"I'm only asking," the garden fairy replied. "And I think it's a fair question.

If Gabby doesn't care about her shadow, there's no sense wasting time trying to find it. We only have so much fairy dust, and we still need to find Tinker Bell."

Everyone looked at Gabby. "It's up to you," Iridessa told her.

Gabby thought about it. What was a shadow good for, after all? It wasn't exactly a friend. You couldn't talk to it. Or play games with it, not real games, anyway. You always knew what your shadow would do a second before it did.

But on the other hand, her shadow had always kept her company. And it was a part of her. She thought of the butterfly shadows and how frightened they'd seemed all on their own.

"My shadow's always stuck by me,"

Gabby decided. "I can't just leave it behind."

"All right, then," Rosetta said. "Fawn, tell us again what the bats said about breaking the curse."

"Just what I told you," said Fawn. "They said we have to find that magic stone."

"But did they say where we should look for it?" Lainey asked.

"Or what the magic stone looks like?" Iridessa added.

"Or what we're supposed to do once we find it?" Silvermist chimed in.

"So many questions!" Fawn huffed, folding her arms. "They just said, 'Find the magic stone.' All right?"

"Maybe it will all be clear when we find it," Kate said. "And the sooner we start looking, the better. Think of it like a treasure hunt. I bet that old king hid it somewhere in this castle. For all we know, it's been right under our noses this whole time."

They spread out to search, each taking a different part of the castle. Gabby picked her way through the ruins, examining the rocks and pebbles she found. There were stones everywhere. How would she know when she found the right one?

She picked up a small stone with golden flecks in it. *Could this be it?* Gabby wondered. *Or what about this one shaped like a heart? Or this one with the milky stripe running through it?*

None of them seemed particularly magical. But

she put them all in a pile, just in case.

The day wore on. Gabby's pile grew. But each stone she added only made her doubt the others. She felt as if she was going in circles. What had Mia called it?

A wild-goose chase, Gabby remembered.

That made her think of the funny moth. She realized she hadn't seen it since the day before. Not since she'd passed through the arch.

Gabby straightened up. The rocks she was holding fell from her hands.

The moth had been trying to warn her. It had tried to keep her from passing through.

"I know where we need to look!" she cried.

Her friends came running at the

sound of her yell. "What is it?" Kate asked breathlessly. "Did you find it?"

"Follow me," Gabby said.

She led them across the castle grounds toward the arch.

"This is where my shadow came off. So this must be where the curse is. Maybe the stone is here, too," Gabby suggested.

They searched all around the arch, but they didn't find anything other than the most ordinary-looking stones.

Kate was about to step under the arch to look beneath it. But Iridessa stopped her just in time.

"If we're right and this is where the curse is, you can't walk beneath it, or you'll lose your shadow, too." The fairy turned to Gabby. "You'll have to be the one who searches it."

Gabby stepped up to the arch. She'd already lost her shadow when she stepped through it. What might she lose this time?

Gabby took a deep breath and walked under it. To her great relief, nothing happened.

"Look around," Mia urged her. "Do you see anything that could be a magic stone?"

Gabby looked up at the arch curving over her head. It was made of rectangular stones, piled one on top of the other.

In the center, at the very top of the arch, was a wedge-shaped stone. And on the underside of the stone, she saw a small dark circle.

"There's something up there!" Gabby exclaimed. "But I can't see it from here. I need fairy dust to fly up."

She came out of the arch, and Fawn sprinkled her with fairy dust. As soon as the fairy dust settled on her, Gabby felt its magic working. As she started back to the arch, her feet were already leaving the ground.

But before she could fly up to the top, something small and dark whipped past her face. Gabby looked around, startled.

The moth was back!

"There you are!" Gabby felt strangely pleased to see it. "I was hoping you'd come back."

Of course, the moth didn't reply. It was buzzing frantically around her. For the first time, Gabby got a good look at it. Up close, it didn't look much like a moth at all. It looked like a fairy—

if a fairy had been made entirely of smoke.

It's not a moth, Gabby thought. *It's a shadow. A fairy's shadow!*

The shadow turned more urgent circles. It was trying to tell her something.

"What? What is it?" Gabby looked toward the woods, where the shadow was pointing. Her heart gave a leap.

There, at the edge of the woods just

beyond the arch, was Gabby's shadow.

Gabby called out to it. But her shadow never turned in her direction. It was looking over its shoulder at something among the trees. What Gabby saw then made her knees go weak.

Another shadow was behind her own. This shadow was much bigger than Gabby's. Bigger than a tree—no, bigger than a house! It emerged from the woods, growing larger and larger. Like a great dark cloud, it seemed to pull all the light with it.

Gabby's scream stuck in her throat as she stared up at the great shadow beast.

Chapter 9

When Iridessa saw the huge shadow come out of the forest, she recognized it at once. It was the same awful thing she'd seen in the night.

But how much more terrible it looked in the daylight!

The shadow crept forward on dozens of legs. Wings sprouted from its head. Horns grew out if its back. A tail as thick as a tree trunk dragged behind it. But the most frightening part was its center. It was like a big black hole.

With frightened cries, the girls and fairies turned to flee.

But as the shadow beast lurched toward them, Iridessa paused. There was something odd about the beast's movement. It limped along in a herky-jerky way, as if it was being pulled in several directions at once.

Iridessa's heart pounded with fear. Her body wanted to fly away. But she made herself look closer.

She saw that the beast's wings resembled the wings of an eagle. Its many legs were long and rangy, like the legs of wolves. And its thick tail whipped unhappily like a trapped snake.

Or many snakes. The butterfly shadows sprang into Iridessa's mind.

Shadows are not always what they seem.

Suddenly, she understood. This beast wasn't a monster. It wasn't even a beast. It was a bunch of lost, trapped shadows. And they needed her help.

There was no time to collect sunbeams. This time Iridessa would have to be the sun.

Iridessa took a deep breath and flared her glow. Bright, brighter, brightest, until she shone like a tiny star.

Then, like a blazing arrow, she flew straight at the heart of the beast.

She heard Gabby cry, "Iridessa! No!" But there was no stopping now. A second later, Iridessa plunged into inky blackness.

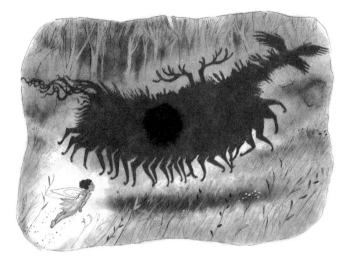

Iridessa had never been in darkness
so complete. It felt as if a black cloth had
been thrown over her, muffling all her
senses. Although she knew that she was
blazing, she couldn't see her own light. For
a moment, she feared she wasn't strong
enough. Maybe even the power of fairy
magic wasn't enough to help the shadows.

But she had to try!

Iridessa closed her eyes and shone with all her might.

From inside the beast, Iridessa could not see what was happening. But her friends saw. As the fairy's light pierced the shadows, the shadow beast began to come apart.

The beast's wings broke away and became the shadow of a hawk. It hovered for a moment, wings spread wide, as if relishing its freedom. Then it soared away into the sky.

The beast's horns came off next. The shadow of a stag bounded away, kicking its legs high with joy.

The beast's legs peeled away and became a pack of wolf shadows. They slinked

off into the forest, disappearing
among the trees.

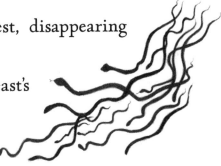

The shadow beast's
tail broke into
the shapes
of a dozen
snakes. They slithered into holes in the
ground and vanished.

One by one, faster and faster, the
shadows peeled away. Out came the
shadows of rabbits, crows, and raccoons.

Still, Iridessa blazed on. The beast
shrank and shrank, until there was only
a single shadow left—the shadow of a tiny
mouse.

The mouse shadow lifted its head
and sniffed the air, as if amazed by this
sudden change. Then it scurried off.

The shadows were all gone. Iridessa was left alone, her glow now nothing but a faint gleam.

She wobbled in the air for a second. Then she sank to the ground. Her glow winked out.

*

When Iridessa opened her eyes, the first thing she saw was Kate, Mia, Lainey, and Gabby leaning over her. Their big faces blocked out the sky.

"She's awake!" Mia exclaimed.

"Stand back, everybody. Give her some room," Rosetta commanded. The fairies came buzzing through, clearing the girls out of the way.

Silvermist placed a cool hand on

Iridessa's forehead and asked, "How are you feeling?"

"A little tired," Iridessa replied. The truth was, she felt as if she could sleep for a hundred years. "How long was I out?"

"Only a few minutes. Here, this ought to make you feel better." Fawn sprinkled a hefty handful of fairy dust over Iridessa.

At once, Iridessa felt better, stronger. She could feel her glow returning.

"Iridessa!" Kate exclaimed. "That was so cool! You were like—*wow!*" Kate spread her fingers like the rays of a sun. "And that beast just came apart. How did you know it would do that?"

"The butterflies," Iridessa said. "When I saw the shadow beast, I guessed maybe the same thing happened—that it was just a bunch of lost shadows. Over the years, different animals must have come through here. When they passed through the arch, they lost their shadows. The shadows grouped together for comfort, and then they couldn't get apart. I think that's how the beast came to be."

Iridessa thought for a moment. Then she added, "I guess shadows don't really like to be alone. It's their nature to be attached."

"I got my shadow back." Gabby said, stepping forward. Now Iridessa could see Gabby's shadow standing beside her, like a ghostly twin. "But I can't figure out how to get it back on."

"Was your shadow part of the beast, too?" Iridessa asked.

Gabby shook her head. "I thought so at

first. But I think my shadow led the beast to us. It knew that we could help."

"Clever shadow," Iridessa said. "Just like her girl."

"What will happen to all those other shadows?" Lainey asked. "Will they find their animals again?"

"Not until the curse is undone," Fawn said. "At least, that's what the bats told us."

"I almost forgot—the magic stone!" Gabby flew up to the top of the arch. They saw her reach under the keystone and feel around.

Her face fell. "It's not there."

"Are you sure?" Kate asked.

"I'm sure," Gabby said. "I can feel a hole, but there's nothing in it. Whatever was there is gone."

A groan of disappointment went

around the group. "That means someone else got the stone first," Mia said.

"And I think I know who it could have been," said Gabby. "Tinker Bell!"

chapter 10

"Tinker Bell?" the others exclaimed in unison.

"Gabby," Mia said, "didn't we agree you wouldn't say anything about Tinker Bell unless you were sure—"

Gabby cut her off. "I'm sure." Then she turned to look up into the trees. "Hey, come out!" she called. "Don't be afraid."

For a moment, nothing happened. Then a small dark shape flitted down from the treetops, darting like a nervous hummingbird. Only when it stopped right in front of them could everyone see it clearly.

"It's Tink's shadow!" Iridessa exclaimed with a gasp.

The shadow put a fist on its hip. It cocked its head as if to say, *No kidding.*

"I've seen it before!" Silvermist said, realizing. "On the Lost Coast! I thought I saw a spirit in the fog. But it wasn't a spirit. It was Tink's *shadow!*"

"I saw it, too!" Fawn exclaimed. "That night by the campfire. Tink's shadow was on the rock. I thought my eyes were playing tricks on me."

Tink's shadow sighed heavily. If it had had a face, it would have been rolling its eyes.

"It really does look like Tinker Bell," Rosetta remarked.

"It's been following us for a long time," Gabby told them. "I thought it was a moth at first."

"If Tink lost her shadow, that means she must have come this way, too," Kate said. "So we're on the right trail. But where is she now?"

Tink's shadow shrugged.

"I think that's why it's been following us," Gabby explained. "The shadow is hoping we'll lead it back to Tink."

Tink's shadow nodded.

"But if Tinker Bell really does have the magic stone, why is her shadow here?" Lainey asked. "Shouldn't it be with *her*?"

"Something must have happened," Mia said. "There must be a reason she couldn't undo the curse."

Everyone went quiet, thinking about what this could mean. In the silence, Gabby became aware of a faint sound. She lifted her head. "Do you hear that?" she asked.

"I don't hear anything," Kate said.

"Wait . . . listen. I hear it, too," Mia said. "It sounds like a bell."

From far off came a slow, rhythmic clanging. The sound was deep and a little sad.

"It's the sound I heard last night!" Gabby said. She turned to Iridessa. "I wasn't dreaming. I really did hear it."

"But what is it?" asked Rosetta.

"Oh!" Mia said. "Look at Tinker Bell's shadow!"

The sound seemed to have an electric effect on the fairy shadow. It cocked its head and listened, trembling like a leaf in the wind. Its wings moved so fast they were only a blur.

Suddenly, without warning, it darted away.

"Quick! Follow it!" Kate exclaimed.

They scrambled after the shadow. It wasn't easy to follow, because every time it came to a patch of shade, it disappeared. Then they had to look everywhere until someone spotted it again.

The shadow led them all the way to the edge of the cliff. There it stopped, looking out at the sea.

The girls and fairies skidded to a stop behind it. They peered out at the whitecapped waves. Fog was rolling in, making it difficult to see.

"I don't understand. Why did her shadow lead us here?" Lainey asked.

They could hear waves crashing on the rocks below. And something else.

"Listen!" Kate cried. "It's the bell again." The sound rolled toward them on the wind, slow and sad.

Clang-clang.

Clang-clang.

Standing above the sea, they suddenly made sense of the sound. It was the clang of a ship's bell. But where was the ship?

They were all looking at the water. So if Gabby hadn't happened to glance up,

she would have missed it. Far off shore, a
shape appeared in the fog. At first Gabby
thought it was a bird. But as it came closer,
she made out the shape of a wooden prow
and a tiny sail.

"Look! There!" she pointed.

"It can't be . . . ," Kate said.

"It is! It's a boat!" Lainey cried.

"Not just *any* boat," Mia said. "It's the *Treasure*!"

The little boat sailed across the rolling fog, like a ship riding the waves. From where they stood on shore, they could just make out a small light on board—a light that could have been a fairy's glow.

"I see Tink!" Gabby cried. "I really do this time!"

"But what's she doing way up there?" asked Mia.

Fawn slapped her forehead. "Why didn't I think of it? We've been looking for Tink in the wrong places. We were following the river and looking for her boat along the coast. But Tink doesn't need water to sail that boat. She has loads of fairy dust! She can fly!"

They watched the tiny boat come closer. It looked as if it was struggling. It was tossed up and down on the wind. Its mast tilted dangerously to one side.

The girls jumped up and down, waving their arms. They yelled Tinker Bell's name.

But if Tink heard them, she gave no sign. Suddenly, the boat made an abrupt turn and disappeared into a patch of fog.

"Where is she going? Why is she leaving?" Lainey asked.

"Tink! Tink!" they cried louder. But the boat was gone. The sound of the ship's bell faded away.

"Didn't she see us?" Gabby cried in dismay.

Iridessa looked troubled. "I had the feeling she did. It seemed as if she turned *because* she saw us."

"But we're her best friends. Why would she run away?" Rosetta asked.

"Well, we're not going to figure it out standing here," Kate said, lifting her chin. She looked out at the sea of fog, narrowing her eyes against the wind. "We came here to find Tinker Bell. And that's what we're going to do."

Kate held out her hands. Gabby took one. Lainey grasped the other. Mia took Gabby's free hand. The fairies joined hands, too. Tink's shadow hovered close by, as if afraid to be left behind.

"Everybody ready?" Kate asked.

"Ready," said Mia, Lainey, and Gabby. They squeezed each others' hands.

"Ready," said Silvermist, Iridessa, and Rosetta.

"Let's finish this quest," Fawn added.

Still holding hands, the girls rose off the cliff and plunged into the swirling mist. This time, no matter what, they were going to find Tink.